WATERS

Edith Newlin Chase

Ron Broda

Scholastic Canada Ltd.

Sprinkling, wrinkling,
softly tinkling,

twinkling tiny brook,

running, funning,
hiding, sunning,

cunning baby brook,

joins a grown-up brook.

11

Dashing, splashing,
sunlight flashing,
stony grown-up brook,

13

joins the river,
broad smooth river,

deep as deep can be.

Slower, slower, slower flowing,

wider, wider, wider growing,

till it empties all its waters out
into the great huge sea.

Rolling, rolling,
tossing, rolling,

splashing waves forever rolling
in the great wide sea.

To Lyra and Larsson,
Michael and Isobel,
and other children who love
streams and the sea.
E.N.C

For my brothers and sisters:
Bob, Tom, Terry, Connie, Crystal,
Fred, Kevin, Kim, Todd and Brigit.
Also in loving memory of our father,
Fred Broda.
R.B.

Photography by William Kuryluk.
The illustrations for this book were done with paper
sculpture and watercolour. Each layer was cut, formed
and painted before being glued into place.

No part of this publication may be reproduced or stored in a retrieval system, or transmitted in any form or by any means, electronic, mechanical, recording, or otherwise, without written permission of the publisher, Scholastic Canada Ltd., 123 Newkirk Road, Richmond Hill, Ontario, Canada L4C 3G5. In the case of photocopying or other reprographic copying, a licence must be obtained from CANCOPY (Canadian Reprography Collective), 214 King Street West, Suite 312, Toronto, Ontario, M5H 3S6.

6 5 4 3 2 1   Printed in Hong Kong   4 5 6 7 8/9

Canadian Cataloguing in Publication Data

Chase, Edith Newlin
Waters

Poems.
ISBN 0-590-74201-9

I. Water – Juvenile poetry. 2. Children's poetry, American. I. Broda, Ron. II. Title.

PZ8.3.C358Wa 1994   j811'.54   C94-930928-1